PARALLELS COULD MEET

MEDHA SUNEJA

Contents

CHAPTER I

Surprise

"Do you believe it finally happened" said Brad with his cheeky little smile.

"Yeah I mean how fast is everything changing" I replied with a excited tone but deep down I was really pissed off.

Everyone around me was so elated but something was bothering me. It was our graduation day and we were looking forward for starting a new phase of our life and by 'we' I mean our gang. From the very first day of the college, we stick together as best friends , and soon became a close family.

So the reason I was so dolorous was that our student life was about to end , there would be so less time for us to spend with each other , we all had different roads to travel and our steps would no longer collide in this town as they used to everyday.

Brad was applying for a job in New Jersey , Shane was planning to be a part of a wildlife magazine as a photographer which also means he have to start his new phase of life in woods which according to me sucks . As expected , Noah was going to accompany his father in their tourism business. Jaelyn would open her own store with her own collection of designer clothes and her am I , Tracy , not knowing where my life is leading , everybody got plans for their future and I am still deciding what to eat for lunch today.

Nevermind, in addition to it , I still can't digest the thought of us going our separate ways and meeting once in a year or something like every friend group at some point face. These are the people with whom I spent most of my last 6 years and I just don't want to let them go.

My phone beeped and I got a message from my mom which says "Hi ! I just sent you a number of an agency , just talk to them and fix a date for an interview. It is for the post of an editor in local newspaper". I left her on seen , because I was not even sure if I wanted to do that interview or anything.

" I got a good news" said Noah.

"What is it ? " I asked him.

" You are going to have to wait for it . Just meet me at the Vastar Cafe at 6PM , I have asked everybody to come . Don't forget."

And then he disappeared in the crowd . I was wondering what he was going to say but atleast I got something to look forward to other than sobbing on the couch tonight and watching Netflix. I decided to go there little earlier as today I wasn't in the mood to hear taunt from Brad that I am always a latecomer.

When I reached there , Jaelyn was already sitting in our usual booth drinking her usual coffee. I sat beside her and asked if she knows anything about Noah's news. She nodded her head no, which made me a little concerned as they both share everything with each other like every small detail keeping in mind they are dating for last 2 years and still going strong .

" I literally asked him 10 times but he didn't open his mouth at all. I feel maybe there's something wrong with him or like he is tensed " said Jaelyn with a sign face .

" Nah, I don't think that's the case , he said it's a good news! Just wait for him ", I said simply.

Meanwhile , Shane and Brad also reached but there was no trace of Noah.

" Damn ! It's almost 6:30 PM , this idiot is making me so mad , What's the freaking news ? I feel like he is just pranking with us and he is not going to come , he is not even answering his phone " said Brad angrily.

" He's not a 10- year old to pull a prank like this . Just wait he must be stuck somewhere" Shane replied with a relaxed tone .

Brad was always like this , he had no patience and sometimes it's hard to control him when he's angry and maybe that's the reason we aren't together anymore . When we were dating, soon our relationship became a toxic one so we called it off and we realised we were better off as friends than partners .

As we were talking , I saw Noah entering the cafe and walking to us.

" Finally ! The almighty has come. Do you need anything, Sir ? You must be so tired by making us wait here for almost an hour " said Brad sarcastically.

"Vodka would work " Noah replied.

Well this make Brad really pissed but I enjoyed the look on his face .

" Okay, so what's the matter , Naoh ? "

" Relax Jaelyn , let me make myself comfortable first , I just came"

It literally took him 20 more minutes to get comfortable as he was playing with our patience level and I swear to god I would have walked out if he'd stayed quiet for a minute more .

" So as you all know , I'm joining my Dad's tourism business and I decided that the first trip which I'm going to plan will be ours. We are all going to Europe next weekend , so pack your bags guys. A Private Jet plane , beaches , best hotel rooms are waiting for you " Noah said finally!!

Well, the news was more than good. Maybe that's going to be our last trip together and Noah literally us jump of our seats with excitement as we haven't gone to a place that far before. We just hoped it's going to be an amazing one and then we raised our glasses to cheers .

1 Week later

Well, there are some advantages of a rich friend for sure. So our flight was near about of 7 hours , and we all were ready for one hell of a ride.

While we are just about to leave for the airport , we got a news that huge winds were blowing over Atlantic Ocean and it is kinda risky to travel at that time. After 17 hours when the winds were mid , we decided to start our beautiful journey or you can say an unforgettable one .

Noah had booked a private plane so there were only 10 people boarding the flight - us five , two pilots , two air hostesses and one unknown person who was a dear friend of the owner of the plane . By the way , he looked really mysterious and not for a second had he moved his eyes from the window of the plane . We tried talking to him but he was like a weird freak and doesn't even bothered to reply.

We ignored him and started gossiping about other things but I can't get him off my mind like how could someone could remain as rock for more than an hour without moving a finger . He could have won tournaments of the famous game - " Green light , Red light " if there were any .

CHAPTER II

Weird Freak

Jennie , our air hostess , tried to offer some food to that weird guy but he just signed no without losing the sight of the clouds from the window.

I got to know from Noah that he was some kind of a scientist , who was working on a big project in London. Well , his career was quite impressive but in person he seemed rude and kinda nerd.

We all were taking about what we were going to do when we landed there. Suddenly we felt something like a big rock hit the plane. There was a little turbulence but no damage was seen on plane as it was flying smoothly.

" What was that ?" exclaimed Shane.

" It felt something like an earthquake"

" Shut up, Brad! We are in air , how could there be an earthquake up here "

" You never know , Shane. Anything could be possible like who could have imagined you would pass the finals but you did right . I still can't believe it tho ! "

" Gosh ! That thing was a practical but this isn't"

" Blah ! Blah ! Whatever "

" Would you guys ever stop fighting " said Jaelyn " You are really like dog and cat who just want to kill each other and looking for a perfect moment for it "

" Well, then I'd be dog " said Brad

" Whatever , Just go and ask the pilot if everything is alright' said Shane.

" I think God has given you a mouth and working legs to go to the pilot room and asked them yourself " replied Brad .

" Stop you both , I just talked to the pilot and everything is fine. They can't figure out what really was that but by God grace the plane is in good condition " exclaimed Noah .

We were flying over Atlantic Ocean , Shane and Brad were still fighting over dogs are better or cats as Jaelyn referred it to them. They both fight with each other a lot but at the end of the day they still care for each other.

Then nearly after 15 minutes , we again felt the same thing , everyone was confused what really was happening but that weird freak still didn't even move a little.

" What the hell is happening ? " said Brad.

" Wait , lemme check "

" Noah , are you trying to kill us . I already know you'd be the reason of my death someday "

" Brad , for once, can you speak things which are relevant "

" But you planned out the trip and you don't even have the answer about why is this happening"

" Ignore him and see what the pilot said " said Jaelyn

" How can he see what the pilot said , ask him to hear " said Brad

" Don't say a word more or I'm going to smack your head on the wall" Said Jaelyn aggressively.

Noah came after a little while and almost gave us a mini heart attack as he told us that our plane had lost connection with the control room. Never in my life , I had imagined something like this happening to me. We thought maybe it was because of weather due to which our flight was delayed earlier but according to the pilots , weather seems quite good now.

" The pilots are trying to connect with control room so that our plane could land at some nearby airport " said Noah nervously.

" Just pray that some miracle happens" I said

Well , after I completed saying this , some miracle did happen , huge freaking thunderstorms. Gosh ! Never in my life I had said something and it got fulfilled but now it did but in a negative way rather than positive.

" Congratulations, God heard your prayers , Tracy, and gave us this miracle thunderstorm keeping in mind that there were no chances of this 1 minute ago " said Brad .

" Well , if God is hearing my prayer I should pray that this thunderstorm take you out from this plane and throw you to a mental hospital because you never know when to be serious" I said angrily.

" I'd rather be at mental hospital than being here with you "

" Brad , it seems that you are always ready to pick up a fight with anyone " said Jaelyn

" And it seems like you are always ready to poke your nose in my fights " replied Brad savagely.

Meanwhile , we completely forgot about that freak and when I tried to take a look at his seat , I noticed he was not there .

" Where did that guy go " I asked Jennie

" He must have gone to washroom "

So he is a human . Then something struck in my mind that thunderstorm started when he was in washroom and before that weather was all clear when he was sitting here. Maybe I was just overthinking as I have never faced situations like this earlier. Well no one else has too. I was having a very odd feeling about that guy.

I prayed that it wasn't something like that but wait I shouldn't have prayed because God was also playing games with me .

After some time , we again felt it , it was happening continuously in gap of every 10 minutes. Then I felt that someone was holding my hand so tight , I looked back and noticed it was Jaelyn and she was having a panic attack. Noah immediately brought some water for her and we all tried to keep her calm. It wasn't the first time she was having panic attack , she used to have these continuous attacks till she became 10 . From the last 6 years , had I known her , I saw her having it only thrice in situations when she get so much tensed and it was one of that . Noah gave her required medicines which she always used to carry with herself and after taking it she became a bit relaxed and Noah gave her a tight hug and anyone could see the love they had for each other.

" It's getting worse , what should we do now ? " Asked Shane while breathing heavily.

" There's no other option than to wait " I said

" Wait for what ? A other miracle which you are going to pray for"

Said Brad as expected

" Wish I could just put a tape on your mouth"

" Who's stopping you, do it now "

" If I had it , I would have done it so earlier only "

" Huhh , like you could "

" BTW , that weird guy is in washroom from last 30 minutes " I said

" He must have eaten something heavy " said Brad

" No Brad , it's something else "

" Why'd you care so much about that guy ? Do you like him?"

" Literally , please just shut up and use your mind if you have any . He was acting so differently from starting"

" So you are trying to say that he is making all those earthquakes ? "

" It's not an earthquake , IDIOT ! How many times should I tell you"

" Don't get me started Shane and just sit quietly " said Brad

" She actually got a point " said Noah

" Oh ! Now you also believed her stupid theory , Why can't you understand it's not a work of a single person" said Brad

" Nobody asked for your opinion , let's talk to him , he's a scientist , maybe he has an idea about what the hell is happening on plane " said Shane

" Okay , Do whatever you want " said Brad

CHAPTER III

Is This Hell ?

We asked Jennie , if that guy is going to take more time but she said that he was not responding as she knocked the washroom door twice.

" See , now that's so strange" said Jaelyn

" Nothing's strange , he must be sleeping there because Shane was snoring so loud , so he had to go to washroom to take a peaceful nap " said Brad.

" I only slept for 10 mins and then that thing happened which you called an earthquake "

" 10 mins are more than enough to terrify a person "

" Let me look for the emergency key of the washroom " said Jennie

" Oh ! Thank you for thinking about it so much earlier "

" Sorry Brad , I had forgotten about it "

Thunderstorm was getting more terrible and the rocks like structure keep on felling on the plane continuously. At first , we thought it was maybe due to storm but pilots believed it was not possible for a Strom like this to carry that large stones at this height .

Jennie brought the keys and then we tried to open the door .

" Do it fast , Jennie " Said Noah

" I m doing it , Noah "

Then finally the door get opened and that man was just standing there with a remote like device in his hands .

He was wearing an evil smile which literally scared the shit out of me

" Come out here fast " said Shane

He came out and suddenly burst into laughter with tears like he has achieved something that he was trying for so long.

" Gosh ! I knew something was up with this creature "

" Why are you laughing like that ? " asked Jaelyn

" No , he is crying, there are tears " said Brad.

" Not now Brad , not now " replied Jaelyn

He tilted his eyes towards the left and suddenly the plane lost control and balance and it's just suddenly started moving in circles. And then I black out .

As we must have heard the story that when a person experienced his near death experience he only think about the person whom he love the most , same happened with me , when plane get crashed , I saw my parents but to my surprise I also saw Noah , he was just staring at me and I felt like If I'm gonna die today , I just want him beside me and I just can't ignore this feeling , maybe it was due to so much stress I was taking and there's no logic behind it because Noah and Jaelyn are perfect together and just made for each other.

When my eyes opened, it was all dark . I don't remember anything happened to me after that guy tilt his eyes in that crazy way .

My leg was hurting like hell and I wasn't even able to stand on my own.

" Are you guys here ? I m not able to see anything "

I screamed loudly , hoping my gang was around only but then I heard some noise of heavy breathing and I literally got chills .

" Who's this ?"

I kinda heard a familiar voice coming from back and it calmed my soul.

" Tracy , is this you , are you fine ? "

" Noah , Thank God you are here ! "

I gave him a really tight hug because for a second I thought I'm never gonna see him again and that specific moment is captured in my heart for forever.

" Do you remember anything how we reached here , it's all so blurry in my head " asked Noah

" I only could think of the moment when that guy did some eye movement and plane started to lose its control , and then I don't know what happened to us and how we reached here "

" Do you have any idea where others are , I been trying to find them for so long ?"

" Nope , I just opened my eyes , I don't know from how many hours I have been here "

" Okay , but now let's find others too "

" How could we , it's all dark , there could be ditches around here and what else we can't really figure that out "

" Do one thing , try to crawl and we will scream their names while moving , maybe they are around only and just be careful and hold my hand "

" Yeah , let's do this "

Sticking to the same ,we crawled all through the dark , screaming our friend's names at top of our lungs but failed to find anybody. We tried our best , our throat really got dry and also start paining due to continuous screaming from the last few hours. We were losing our hope as we got so tired , were thirsty and literally starving. We were crying for held but nothing was happening , we didn't even had our phones to connect with our parents. Just two people stuck in this hell like place hoping to be found. We weren't in a situation to talk or walk more so we decided to take a little nap to get some energy.

I wake up not knowing how many hours I've slept again and wasn't even sure if it's daytime or night as there was no single ray of light. Few moments later , Noah too woke up and we tried to walked more miles but it was seemed like a never ending journey. As we were moving forward to god knows where we felt something .

" This is water right ? " Said Noah and I nodded yes instead of having doubts that it could also be blood cause the place we were in feels like bloody hell only.

But eventually it was water only .

" Finally , we atleast found something , at this moment this water really feels like gold . It's coming from left , let's move in that direction " I said.

Water level kept on increasing as we move forward towards it until we reached a point where water was almost the level of our chest and there's no way we could go ahead and also we didn't even know how to swim. Water seems quite fresh and we dranked it till our body which is almost 70% water became 90% as we were really thirsty and there was a drought in our throats. It really sucked when we followed water for almost an hour hoping to found something but coming empty handed but yeah atleast we got some water .

" We are just going round and round to nothing and currently is on same stage where we were few hours ago"

"Relax Tracy ! We would find a way through the dark , Do you believe me ?"

" I believe you more than I believe myself "

" Great , so just take a deep breath and follow my lead and don't worry , I'm here with you , Now just litsen to me , let's try going towards right maybe we will find something that side "

" I have a leg pain because of that crash maybe , can we just rest for few minutes , I'm not able to walk further ? "

" Yeah , why not , I'm tired too " said Noah

" It's really crazy , like we should have been in Europe currently if that thing didn't occur but here we are , and it all happened in just a span of few hours"

" That's life dude , it never went in the way we actually wanted , it got its own plans "

" Do you think the rest are alive ? "

" I guess so , if we are maybe they are too. I'm just thinking about them only. "

" Through the course of last few years , we've become a kind of family , I'm more close and open to you guys than to my own parents."

" I know right , I mean I couldn't even imagine my life without our stupid talks, those weird pranks we used to pull out , those late light gossips , kicking around the town , long sleepovers , hilarious fights and what not "

" Do you remember the day when we were in 2nd year and we beat that topper guy because he was bullying Shane and messing with us , due to which we got suspended from the college for the rest of the month ?"

" Ofcourse ! How could I forget that , it was such a good time , we didn't even had to do any assignments and were just chilling around for the whole month "

" Hahaha , and you joined gym that same day so that when again fight like this happens you don't need Brad's help but you left it the 2nd day "

" Yeah , my body doesn't support that thing , and it's really sucked carrying all those weights instead I could have made body by carrying Jaelyn"

" Lol , yeah that could have been a great help "

" Today , I promise you one thing , if we will make it out alive , I'll be always with you guys no matter what till my dying breath and will never leave your side "

" I promise the same to you "

With that promise, we again started walking towards right direction in hope to find something helpful.

CHAPTER IV

One Step Away To Enter

While we were moving forward , we heard a computerized voice which keep on repeating. We followed the voice and when we reached near it , the voice became more clear and clear.

" You are one step away to enter " This was the exact words.

" It's coming from there " I said

" Yeah , let's make no noise and see if anyone's there "

When we reached there , we hide under a stone like structure and in front of us there was something which can't be described through words. It was something like a hole in the air and different colors of beam was coming out of it. The man was standing there with the same remote in his hands moving his fingers through it .

" Finally , we found him. Now you just see what I am going to do with him "

" Wait , be calm Noah , he is the only person who can let us out from here. "

" Yeah , but he is the reason why we're here "

" I know that , but he could be armed . We should be careful regarding our next move. There could be worse consequences "

" Yeah, you are correct "

It was hard for us to come up with a idea to tackle him. We weren't in best of our health, haven't eaten something from so long already had weakened us.

" Tracy , there's someone on the left corner of that hole "

" I couldn't see anything beyond that hole , it's all dark "

" I am sure there is definitely someone , maybe it's one of our friends "

" Then without making a noise , we should go there from behind "

" No , you have to stay here , I'll go . I can't put you at risk "

" And you think , I will let you go there alone in the Lion's den "

" Please don't argue with me , let me go."

" Ok then , none of us would go there "

" So , you mean to say , we should just stay here and do nothing and let that man complete his work"

" I am not ready to hear anything . I have make my mind either it's both of us or none of us. "

" You are so stubborn !! "

" So , what you have decided ? "

" We'll both go then , you had left me with no choice"

" Good , let's go then "

We decide the we would crawl very slowly so that he couldn't notice us. Noah was correct , there really was a person . As we reached near , we reliased it was our air hostess , Jennie .

" It's Jennie ,her hands and legs are tied up with rope and there's tape on her mouth. " Whisperd Noah

We opened her hands and legs.

" Hey Jennie , it's us , are you okay ? "

" What are you doing here , Eric will saw us , go away" said Jennie.

" Who's Eric ? "

" That man , obviously . He's not a safe person to be around of "

" Jennie , just follow us quietly . He won't notice anything "

We took Jennie to the back where Eric can't hear us.

" What he did to you ? " Asked Noah

" Tell us everything from beginning " I said.

" I don't remember properly , it's all faded in my memory ."

" Try to think hard , please "

" I'm all dazed and confused. I could only remember some bits but not proper scene "

" Yeah , that's okay , just say ? "

" I saw him forcing the other air hostess , Perrie , to go into some kind of hole and she was screaming so loud . I tried to stop him but he pushed me away. I fell over something so hard and fainted. "

" Do you know what's inside that hole ?"

" No , but I saw the pilots before I spaced out. They were tear-eyed as they want to tell me something ."

" You heard them saying something ? "

" I don't think so. They were tied up just like me. That's all I know"

" I think we should wait , nothing's good when we hurry . " I said.

I wasn't able to figure about whether it's all real or just a never ending nightmare. At this moment all I could think about is , that I always had hated my old life , but now I want to go back to that time when there's whole different pace my life has taken. I always thought I was a adventurous girl but now I wish I didn't even took the flight at the first place. There was no trace of my friends , rats were jumping in my stomach , and all we could was to wait till the right moment to get to grips with Eric .

" I can't wait anymore "

" I know but , he has kidnap pilots and maybe our friends are too with him . Our every step have a effect over them ."

" Can't we just find a way out of here instead of discussing " Asked Jennie

" Without our friends, never in a million years " I replied.

" If we stay to save them , we would literally die "

" How you could be so insensitive , we can't leave people behind and go on ? "

" I am being practical , Noah. I don't think we could fight with Eric , he flipped the plane and... "

" Stop , if you wanted to go , just do it on your own. We won't leave without others. "

Jennie stayed with us only as who would wander through this hell like place all alone with not knowing where you are leading.

" Okay, I understand your emotions , I am not leaving alone . "

" No , you should . And thank you for understanding our emotions. "

" Actually I got a plan to save them " said Jennie.

" Don't even open your mouth if it's some sort of rubbish idea "

" Tracy , don't be mean . Atleast litsen to it . "

" Okay , shoot the idea then "

" I will go back to the same area where I was tied up and will make weird noises. There are bunch of ropes in that place . Meanwhile you take them and when Eric will come to check me , just hold him from behind . But be certain of one thing , try to keep that remote away from him. That remote have so many features and it could be threatening "

" That's the most random plan anyone have come up with " .

" Oh , is that so Noah , I didn't liked your plan either . But wait , you didn't even have a plan other than waiting here "

" Noah , let's give it a shot . " I said .

" I got a better idea , Tracy. Let's find those pilots , Jennie saw them before she fainted . They must be somewhere near only. We would know more about Eric and will have more people on our side. "

" We are already three, he is alone , let's make a move "

" Count that remote and that hole too , Jennie. He could use them against us . We didn't even know how they work. "

" I don't think , this idea would run."

" If we didn't find them , then we will follow your plan, Jennie"

" What if he sees is ? "

" Don't be negative "

Then we splited , Noah went to the left of that giant hole. Me and Jennie went to right. We decided that if any of us find pilots or our friends , we would take them behind. After searching for almost half and hour , Jennie and I came empty handed. We had high hopes that Noah will come from bright side . Another hour went by and Noah didn't came back , we both could hear each other heartbeat growing faster as time went by .

" I told you guys , my idea was much better. You don't get anything ."

" Are you substituting for Brad ? "

" Yeah , he is the only sensible between you guys "

" Get your eyesight and brain check dude if you think Brad is sensible. "

" What he said on plane that it must be Noah's game make more sense to me now "

" He was just kidding at that moment. I didn't even want to give you an explanation on Noah's kindness and loyalty. He can't even think of doing this. I could trust him with closed eyes. I could once doubt somebody else but no him that he will cause any pain to us ."

" I thought Noah and Jaelyn are together , but now it's seems a different story."

" Nothing's different , I would defend any of my friends if you say shit about them. "

" Oh , really ! "

" I don't want to waste my time here with you, I'm going in direction Noah went . "

" Have you gone nuts , what if you also didn't came back ? "

"Like you care. I am not staying here because of 'what if's '. "

" Can't you think , He must have been found . "

" No , thats not possible."

I had decided that no matter what I won't stop until I found them.

" Tracy , I don't have that much guts ."

" Okay , do what you want but please keep an eye on Eric. And make sure you don't lose sight of him "

Jennie stayed there only . It's actually better she did that otherwise she would have been a headache like Brad.

CHAPTER V

Pyramid ?

While I was going towards that direction , I noticed some thread like structures that keep on increasing in length as I was moving forward. They were literally everywhere and it was so hard to move between them but tried my best .

There was a moment when I got stuck between them and it took a hour to free myself. Soon I saw a tunnel like structure which was stinking so bad that one's nose hair could dry and fall off. I can't even explain how I managed to breathe at that place.

But atleast the threads were not there anymore and I could move easily through the tunnel. When I was halfway through the tunnel and couldn't find Noah , I was just going to back off . But then I felt something below my foot. It was a bracelet , Noah's bracelet. I didn't even take a second to recognise it because I gifted him this. Although I never saw him wear it , even today as I can remember, he was not having this but I was so confused how it was here . I thought he didn't like it and must have thrown somewhere because obviously Jaelyn thought it was outdated.

But it also means , I was going in right way , Noah must have went from here only.

" Noah , please reply if you're here. It's all dark and I'm so scared. God what did I ever did to you "

I screamed that so loudly that if anywhere else would be here ,till now would have became deaf.

Then , a cool breeze touched my cheeks and neck . I started chasing it like a pleasure to ease a pain .

I passed through the tunnel and it was that much cold that one couldn't even feel his fingers.

" Tracy "

" Tracyyy , up here "

" Ohh God ! How you both reached up here? "

" It's a long story , no time to explain " said Shane

" Shane , I am so glad you are alive "

" I am not leaving you in peace anytime soon. "

" You can talk later , just help us come down. Bring that stone here."

"I am coming up . Hold my hand tightly , and come slowly."

" Noah , we've sent you to save our friends not to stuck with them "

" I know , I was trying to help him but these roots are so evil. They got me . "

" Thanks Tracy . I would have been here forever if you won't have came . Just tell me your real identity , it's there a spider woman behind this mask. Like how could you climbed so smoothly."

" I spent most of my childhood in grandpa's farm. There were so many tress which I used to climbed. "

" Do you have to discuss your whole biography here ? " Asked Noah.

" Noah had told me everything , we have to get hold of Eric " .

" Yeah , but how did you reach here and where are Brad and Jaelyn. ? "

" I woke up here only after that crash . I haven't seen anybody . "

" We should move towards the next tunnel then , let's go ."

" No " they both shouted.

" Why , what's the problem in it ? " .

" Sound of a huge animal is coming from there continuously since so long . "

" I didn't hear anything "

" He must got scared of you , even we are "

" See , we once have to check that place too. By hook or by crook , we have to save them."

" Yeah , let's go there Shane , we're being huge jerks. "

The sound got more louder that we weren't able to hear each other too. But to our surprise , only the sound of that animal could be heard but it was not there , we checked the whole thing as far as we could.

" I don't understand where this sound is coming from , neither I could find a huge animal you were talking about"

" I notice one thing , If we just stay quiet there isn't a sound of a pin. But while we talk , we heard this loud noises." I said .

" So there isn't some sort of animal here "

" According to my observation , yes "

" Wait a minute , while me and Shane were tangled between roots , we heard noises from inside. Which means there was someone inside the tunnel at that time because we were outside and after you came even when we were talking , there was no noise coming at that moment "

" We should check every corner of this place , we got a good lead. "

I was checking walls of the tunnel when I reliased one part of it was wet and soft.

" Guys , this part of the wall is very wet , it's so strange as the rest are so solid. "

Shane and Noah started digging that area and our mouth got completely opened when we found that it's a path to a different place. We got there and it was quite different like it the aura was clean and refreshing.

" There's definitely something here , that is why it was hidden in that tunnel wall "

" Walls here are made of limestone , there must be some important purpose to built a place like this which have such a great entrance ."

" It's a pyramid . I have easily figure that out in 10 hours with no way out " said Brad.

" Brad , you are here . I missed you so much. "

" Bro , for once you literally scared me by appearing out of nowhere "

" You are a little girl , Shane "

" Are you fine ? "

" Yeah ,I am. I can't believe you guys found me."

" I can't believe that too " I said .

" Ok , but now on a serious note , why you are so sure it's a pyramid . "

" Actually , I went to Egypt once on a study trip to learn about Pyramids . There I reasearched about it a lot and according to it , we're definitely inside a pyramid . "

" Technically , that's not possible. "

" I know , but look this place is triangular too."

" But how could our plane reach Egypt? "

" Eric literally could do anything. I highly doubt that he is even a real person . "

" Who's Eric ? " said Brad.

" That man on the plane."

" Tracy , you were correct , he was upto something. Btw where is he now ? "

" I have told Jennie to look after him. We must go now . She'll be all alone. "

" What about Jaelyn ? "

" No Idea , we been trying finding her for so long. I got a feeling that maybe Eric has kidnap her like the pilots."

" She isn't in this pyramid , I can assure you that . I have almost checked everything here except that coffin "

" Why didn't you check that ? "

" Are you mad , there could be a mummy inside ? ".

" Mummies are not real Brad , it's just a fake story . We should check that for complete assurance. " Said Noah.

" Ok , but there no chance she'd be here "

" We can't take chances , already this place is full of mysteries. "

We opened that old coffin , there wasn't a hair inside it but we couldn't find its end. It was like a ditch inside a coffin.

" We should go inside it , it will lead us somewhere. ".

" Do you think it's safe , Tracy ? "

" Yeah we don't even now what's inside it " said Brad.

" Let's move back through that wall " said Shane.

" It was tightly closed , nobody would be there inside "

" No guys , ple-".

Brad interrupted me and said that the hole in the wall through which we came is closed and the area is now covered with limestone in just merely few minutes.

" The only way out is now inside the coffin. Come now . "

We went inside the coffin and it feels like we're in a swing. We were going down so fast and to be honest , I really enjoyed the ride.

" It's so fast , my body left my soul behind . "

" Don't be so dramatic , Brad. "

Finally we came out of a pipe and fell over Eric while he was working with his remote.

" Aahh !! Who's this over me ? " Screamed Eric.

Brad was over him , so it's self explanatory how one of Eric's bone got broken.

" Ohh !! I finally found you knucklehead "

" Get away from me , you are killing me with your weight . What kind of food your mom used to give you ? Said Eric.

" I won't until you tell me what's this mess you have spread around . "

" I'll tell you everything , just please leave me , you have already broken my bone. "

" Brad , I have brought this rope , tie him down ."

" How you guys reached the pyramid and found the secret tunnel ? " Said Eric.

" Look , I told you it's a pyramid. We just found it mistakenly. "

We tied his hands and legs. After seeing us , Jennie also came from behind .

" You guys are heros . You catched him finally . I got so bored looking over him playing with his remote." said Jennie.

" Where's the remote ? He shouldn't get it"

" It's with me , Tracy . Don't worry. " Said Noah.

" Eric , do you need special invitation to tell us everything ? "

" If you want to give , I have no problem "

" Shut up " said Noah while Punching him in his mouth so hard that his 2 teeth fell off.

" Now tell everything"

CHAPTER VI

Secrets Unflod

" Don't be oversmart , otherwise be ready to get another pair of teeth down "

" Ok , ask whatever you want " said Eric.

" Are we in Egypt ? How we reach in a pyramid? "

" This place is interconnection of different places of earth. Like pyramid etc , these places are bit mysterious and their is no clue that who formed this. Nobody knows about this and how to reach here except me."

" Where did you came from ? "

" Some place you are not aware of. It's called Version 56.8. "

" Where's this ? "

" I am coming directly to it , it's a different version of your earth. "

" What are you even trying to say ? "

" The Earth where you are living it's a version 28.91. Its almost 30 years behind my earth version. "

" What do you mean by versions ? "

" It's like in our universe , many worlds exist simultaneously. You must heard of the term ' parallel universe '. "

" Yeah , like in movies few times. "

" But it exists in real life too "

" So why you are here ? "

" Well , I am a scientist in my earth's version. We have technology 30 years ahead of you . For research purposes , I decided to connect with other versions and learn about them. During that process , I found a gateway which connects all these worlds. Through that we entered in your version , but I lost my partner halfway through it. Only he knew the method to go back. Due to which I had to stayed here for last 2 years. I try everything to connect with my version but always got failed until I built this remote. "

" What's the use of this remote then ? " Asked Brad.

" It's multipurpose , it was so hard to built with your backward technology but at last I finally was able to did it. This could do many things like finding the right way to enter different worlds. It could also connect with a machine and head it's functions , the same I did with the plane. "

" You are struggling here with this remote since so long , does it even work ? " Asked Jaelyn.

" Well , it definitely requires some patience. It's not built with morden technology which we use , so it takes ages to respond. "

" I don't care about this versions and all , the main question is why are you troubling us ? "

" Because , I actually needed you to reach here "

" What do you actually mean ? "

" According to my research , I had to reach this place at a exact moment and from exact place otherwise I wouldn't have found it. This gate to reach my world only open for once in every 3 years. And today was that day , if I'd missed it , I would've to wait for the next 3 years here only . "

" You didn't actually answer my question presicely , why you need us ? "

" Beacuse at that exact moment , only your plane was flying over Alantic sea. So it was my only means. "

" You are such a great scientist , you have built this amazing remote , why you haven't made your own plane to do all this " said Noah.

" I felt like this would be waste of my prescious time and energy. Why to built when you could easily get one. I gave some temptation to your father's friend and he allowed me to board the plane. People here are so greedy and could do anything for money "

" You could also just jump from the plane , why you crashed the whole thing ? "

" I told you , I needed some people here and you are youngblood , and would be so beneficial for me . "

" Do you really think , we would help you after you destroy our trip ? " I said.

" Yes , for sure. You are bound to help me if you care for your life "

" Be more clear " said Brad.

" Once someone reach here , he can't go back to his earth until 3 years went by . Same happened with me , only my partner knew how we could avoid the 3 years term."

" So we are stuck here ? "

" No , if you help me. We could go to the version from where I came. And I would figure how to send you back. I can't reach their alone without some help , that is why I chose you guys "

" We ain't even scientist , we can't help you "

" Definitely , you could. Just follow what I say ".

" I don't even believe you . Versions and all , I think he is just messing around with us. I should broke his other bones too , then only he will speak the truth " said Brad angrily.

" Don't believe then, without me you will be here in this place for forever. I built this remote which crashed your plane , see that large hole I created and you still think it's all delusional and I am lying. This is something which someone from your world couldn't even think of doing"

" What's the use of this hole ? "

" It will take us to the gate. We are one step away to enter as my remote is saying . "

" That's the same hole , where he forced Perrie to go " said Jennie.

" Yeah , I needed her to check the stability of the hole. But it's not proper till now , she didn't came back . "

" Did she die ? "

" Yeah , obviously. I am still working on it , so that we don't die in between "

" You killed her , how could you do this ? "

" I didn't kill her , I just sent her inside. "

" It's the same thing "

" Don't worry , you will not be hurt like this. She wasn't even much of a asset to us."

" But she was human. Don't you have a heart or does people belonging to your version are heartless ? "

" If you help me quietly without being a protecter of humanity , You guys would be safe . Next I will be using those 2 pilots to check "

" What if they die too ? "

" There's 99% chance that it won't happen "

" What about the remaining 1% ?"

" If you deeply cared about two stranger pilots than I will send you to test it. "

According to Eric , at every step he would need a person so that he could check if the next step is save or not . I didn't thought he would be that inhuman or I could say inalien as he did feels like a alien and he didn't even belonged to our Earth.

" You said you needed us , but you didn't even try to find us. We were at verge of dying. "

" Because I know you guys would found each other and came here to me at that last. I know you won't even try to run without your friends. Again why to waste my energy and time " .

" Where have you hide Jaelyn ? " Asked Noah

" Oh , I knew something was missing here. So it was that girl Jaelyn. I don't know where the hell she is "

" Did you do something with her like you did with Perrie ? "

" No , I didn't . You should have found her till now . "

" Noah , maybe she's with pilots " said Shane .

" She isn't. Pilots are there at that very corner. Go and see if you find her " said Eric.

We went there opened the ropes of pilots , as expected Jaelyn wasn't there

" Have you guys seen Jaelyn ? "

" Who's she ? " Asked one of the pilots.

" She was with us on the flight wearing a blue top if you remember. "

" No , we hadn't seen here . But what this whole this is "

" We will tell you all about it . Right now our priority is to find Jaelyn. " Said Noah

" You shouldn't find her now. There's only 4 hours left we should start the work now otherwise the entrance would be blocked "

" I don't care about the entrance. We ain't going nowhere without her and neither will I open you "

" You will be risking everyone's life because of Jaelyn. I am opening up Eric. He would open the entrance. " Said Jennie.

" Just stop Jennie . I would break this remote if anyone decided to leave Jaelyn behind" said Shane.

" Okay , we would find her first. But keep the remote safe . It's the only source through which I can go to my world. " Said Eric nervously.

" This place is like a sky. How we could find her ? " Said Jennie.

" This remote could help us. " Said Eric.

" Why you didn't tell this earlier "

" Actually you should be glad , I am helping you "

" There's no point to be glad. You are the one you put us in danger . "

" And I am the one saving you too, so that's even now. "

CHAPTER VII

Attention ! Heartbreak Weather

" How to use this remote ? " Asked Noah

" Press that Green button thrice , then press red and blue together of 5 sec , it will start beeping. " Replied Eric

We did the same as he said, the remote started beeping and colorful arrows were formed at different places.

" Just follow the green arrow , it's for human detection outside our radius. But try to do it faster , we got time limit."

Following the green arrow , we reached the same people where Noah and I woked up.

" According to this , Jaelyn would be in that direction , where the water was earlier . "

Finally the arrow took us to Jaelyn . She was fainted , her body was stone cold. We try to rub her body to make her feel calm. We put all our jackets over her. I brought some water from the lake where me and Noah earlier went.

" She is coming back to her senses. Just move away a bit. Let her breathe . " Said Shane

" I am fine now. " Said Jaelyn.

" So glad to hear it . We were really worried about you. I missed you so much " said Noah with teary eyes and a huge smile.

While they both got reunited , and Noah was holding her tightly , it felt like someone was pinching my heart.

" Are you okay , Tracy ? " Said Shane

" What would happen to me ? I am absolutely fine , just worrying about how we will go back home ."

" I know everything , Tracy. The look in your eyes says all. "

" Please , don't tell anyone about this. It's just a stupid feeling that will eventually go away. "

" You can talk to me anytime , I'll be there for you. "

Meanwhile, we asked Brad to took care of Eric. Only 1.5 hours were left and Eric had started working on the gate in our surveillance.

" Why it sounds like Noah and Jaelyn are having a heated argument ? " Said Shane.

" You must have misunderstood something. They just met and are enjoying each other's company ."

" No , stupid. Just go near them and litsen. "

Shane was correct. They were really confronting each other.

" We are in middle of a crisis. And you guys are fighting over silly things "

" Tracy , how you know it's a silly thing ! "

" Obviously , what would be more important currently other than our safety and our evacuation from this place . "

" Yeah , you are absolutely correct. But she didn't understand this and want to pick fights during this time " Said Noah.

" There's nothing new in you taking Tracy's side " said Jaelyn.

" I am agreeing with her, because she is not immature as you are. "

" First tell me , why this quarrel started ? " Said Shane.

" It's just a misunderstanding she has sowed in her mind "

What really ensued was Jaelyn was hurted with the thing that while me and Noah woke up , Jaelyn was just beside us , but we didn't really noticed her due to darkness. She tried calling our names , but she was not able to speak properly as she got panic attack during that time.

" What's my fault in that , I was not in a position where I could saw you due to darkness. " Said Noah.

" Remember once you said , you could just feel me when I am around. But actually you said this cheesy line to wrong person. This was meant for Tracy. "

" Oh my god , have you hit your head with something. I heard Tracy's screaming that is the reason I was able to find her . "

" Please continue your dispute in low voice. I am working on something more relevant than this love triangle. " Said Eric.

" Shut up , Eric , and do this fast. " Said Brad.

" Jaelyn , it's because of panic attacks and anxiety that you are not able to understand the situation we are in . Just cool down a little bit and we will talk later if we remain alive till the end . " Said Noah.

" I know it's your subtlety to change the direction of the conversation. I want to talk now only . You noticed me , I was just near you. I also touched your hands . But you ignored me to get more time with Tracy. "

" Could you actually hear what you are saying ? "

" Yeah , all loud and clear. Maybe if I had heard myself and my feelings earlier , we would not end up like this. You always has prioritise Tracy over me . "

" No Jaelyn, you are just misinterpreting this whole thing. Noah loves you so much. Why can't you see ? " I said

" I have seen it all now ."

" No you haven't , he even disagreed to move forward without you. We all care for you "

" Tracy , Do you remember the day , when we had gone for hiking. Me and you almost slipped from the cliff but Noah saved you first and I would have fell of if Shane didn't have came in time ."

" That was such a long time ago. The rock which I was holding was almost going to break off. He was saving me and also called Shane to help you at the same time "

Jaelyn was not in a state to judge anything. She was just hurting Noah and us through her words. She was bringing up old situations just to proved Noah doesn't care for him .

" I am not in mood to say anything more. You are just believing what you wanted to believe . Just leave me alone now. " Said Noah frustratingly.

Shane also took Jaelyn away from us to soothe her . Eric told us it will took few more minutes until it get ready to be tested again. Noah was feeling heartsick and I tried talking to him.

" How could she even say those things ? I am wondering since how long she would be having these thoughts . "

" She said those things in the heat of the moment. She will realise this soon."

" I wish . I doesn't even know I was hurting her through my actions. Knowingly or unknowingly her heart got broke because of me and my stupidity. "

" Don't blame yourself . You are not the only one at fault. Conversation is the key for a healthy relationship. She could have discussed these things with you if she felt that way. "

"What should I do now ? ".

" Nothing , just gave her some time and space to open her mind "

I was really disturbed by seeing Noah and Jaelyn like this. Deep down I was blaming myself for all this. Maybe what I feel for Noah was reflected through my words and actions which Jaelyn catched.

I talked to Jaelyn regarding this.

" Maybe , you don't see it Tracy . But I did . He never cared for me as much as he did for you. I never said it earlier because I don't want to lose him but now I just got past the weight which was on my heart for so long. "

CHAPTER VIII

Goodbye , Brother

" The hole is ready to be tested. Someone must go inside it now" Eric whispered in my ears.

I asked him if he could find a alternative to test it rather than sending a person and risking his's life. But it wasn't possible to do so. We all discussed about who should go. Eric wanted one of the pilots to go but we were still having second thoughts.

" You just got a minute. Make a decision fast. " Said Eric.

" I am thinking of going to that hole. I don't want to put anyone in danger. And technically , I am responsible for all this. I organised this trip and all of a sudden we all are standing on a one way road because of me. "

" Don't ever say that again. If you will go , we all will follow you inside. So just keep this thought away from your mind that you are going. " Said Shane.

Everyone insisted that he/she will go among us 5. We doesn't want to lose any of us but had no chance.

" I told you guys earlier also , there's a 99% chance of you coming back alive . Anyone of you had to come forward. "

" Why don't you do that , Eric ? " Said Brad

" I don't mind doing it , but if something happens to me , you all will die too . Nobody knows how to solve this puzzle other than me "

We weren't able to come into a conclusion. While we were discussing , Eric pushed one of the pilots inside it. He was also tired and didn't had the energy to fight back. Until we came to confront Eric , the damage was already done.

" What you did this ? "

" You guys were taking so much time which I didn't really have . So I had to do this. Just be grateful that I didn't choose any of you "

" How dare you ? He was my brother. I will not leave you alive " said Paxton , the other pilot.

" I am sorry , but I promise you he will come back . Just cool down a little bit. "

" If he didn't came back , this will be the last day of your life "

Only 1 hour was left for the gate to get closed.

I was receiting every prayer I ever know for the well being of the pilot .

The radar started beeping which was the sign that there is some kind of motion inside the hole. We thought that pilot is alright and coming back because of gravity inside it which we will eventually turn off if the hole is safe to travel by.

5 minutes went by and we didn't get the news we expected. It was more than 15 minutes since the pilot went in and no one could survive there more than exact 12 minutes. Either he would die or came back.

" He's no more ! " Said Eric.

" But he was supposed to come. What about that 99% thing "

" Well Brad , remaining 1% dominated the rest . It was not in my control. "

" So what would you do now ? Send all of us one by one. We shouldn't even have trusted to with this "

" I hope there will be no need for that " said Eric.

" Shut up , shut up , shut upp . You promised me my brother would came back. " Said the other pilot.

" Promises are made just to break only. It's his destiny . Nothing to do with me kiddo "

Litsening to his careless words , Paxton was boiled in anger. He started raining punches and kicks on Eric.

" Save me you fools , otherwise I will push him inside too " screamed Eric.

" Don't even think of doing it . Otherwise I will push your whole family inside it."

The matter was going out of control. We tried to convince both Paxton and Eric but nothing worked.

" We need to tie them both down otherwise there would be another death today. "

" I'll take down Eric and you take care of Paxton. " Said Brad.

" What would I do then ? " Said Shane.

" It would be more than enough if you took care of yourself only. " Said Brad.

" Brad , Stop taking and separate them. "

" As you say , Jaelyn."

As planned , we both tie them tightly. 40 minutes were left. We tried to make them understand that we couldn't change what happened .

" Paxton , we can't even imagine what you are going through currently. You just lost your brother and your actions regarding to respone to it was apparent. But , we can't bring him back now. We will try our best to ensure nobody dies now. For this we have to work as a team. Please understand brother. "

" I apologize to you , I should've taken more care. Just give me one more chance , I would save us . " Said Eric.

Eric again started working on it. With every minute passing by , we were getting more and more nervous. I couldn't even believe it was just couple of hours at that place because it felt like I was there for a decade.

Noah and Jaelyn still weren't talking to each other. Eric gave us some biscuits which he had carried with him. It was our first meal since the flight. At that time , a biscuit for us was had same value like double cheese pizza. Paxton was telling us about the story , how he and his brother used to accompanied each other in every flight. But at this flight of life , his brother left him behind all alone.

CHAPTER IX

Blow The Rules

" It's done. I did it. I won't even need to test it now . " said Eric with a shine in his eyes.

" Are you really sure ? " Asked Jaelyn.

" Absolutely , there isn't a tiny mistake this time. We all will go inside but in pairs in gap of 1 minute "

" Is it necessary to go in pairs ? Can't we all go at the same time or is it your new trick to fool us ? "

" Well Tracy , at a time only 2 persons could enter. So it is necessary. If you had any inconvenience regarding this , you could go alone too. "

" Okay , let's go in pairs then "

" Yeah , choose your partners fast " said Eric.

Noah asked Jaelyn to be his pair but she absolutely declined and decided to go with Shane. So the pairs were as follows :- Jennie and Shane , Paxton and Jennie , Brad wanted to be with Eric as he can't trust him to go alone or with someone weaker than him. Due to this , I had to go with Noah which none of us wanted after all the drama happened.

Eric instructed us everything we should followed inside. He had put many boundations on us and gave us a charter of rules.

Rule 1 :- Don't see backward even for once no matter what as the dimensions inside it change every minute. We would reach somewhere else according to our head movements.

Rule 2 :- Don't stop anywhere . As you stop , it will be regarded as your final destination and you will reach somewhere else.

Rule 3 :- Count each step you take thoroughly. When you complete 56 steps , make sure you don't take next . Just put your other leg on the base and other should be in air for almost 6 seconds. If you counted wrong , you can't reach the correct place.

Rule 4 :- You are the people of version 28.91. Don't count that number . It must be skipped. Otherwise you can't go there again for the rest of your life.

Rule 5 :- Don't talk in between . It will surely distract you. Your only focus should be on the rules and only rules. One small mistake , and damn you are in huge trouble.

Rule 6 :- You will only have 140 seconds to do these things. If you exceed the time limit than even God won't save you.

" I hope everything is clear now. Do you want me to repeat any of the 6 rules ?"

" Have you lost your mind ? How can we keep these many things in our mind ? " Said Brad .

" It's literally so complicated " said Jennie.

" We can go to any other version but why not ours ? " Asked Noah.

" We can't go back to the version from where we enter this place. You need to go to other one and then return to yours. "

" That's up to you if you want to follow these on not . I am going. There's only 25 minutes left . "

" Guys , there's no time left to complain. It's a do or die situation. We have to rolled our dices now . " Said Noah.

" Before going , let's have a group hug . We don't really know if we would meet again or not " I said.

" Don't be negative , Tracy. We would definitely meet "

" Yeah , let's do a hug " said Eric.

" You are not included in this one , Eric . Just stay away . I hate you more than I hate Maths. " Said Jaelyn

For once , I felt bad for Eric when Jaelyn said this but he actually deserved the hatred from us.

Shane and Jaelyn decided that they will go first followed by Jennie and Paxton. At last me and Noah will go.

At the one minute span , each pair went one by one except me and Noah.

" Best of luck , Tracy "

" Same to you "

" Just hold my hand and don't panic. Take care of all the rules . "

" We can do it , Noah "

We took our first step. Inside it , it was all blurry. Muscles like structure of different colors were floating around . Sometimes it was all lighted , and sometimes it was all dark. There was an absolute silence , we can't even heard the footsteps. It was a kind of place , we which no one ever had imagined . Our whole life was upto those 140 seconds. One wrong step , would have completely changed our future. I never counted something so seriously like I did when counting the steps.

Exactly at the 56th step we did what we supposed to do . Suddenly the floor started moving at a high speed that I can't see what's in front of me. I saw so many earth like planets and it took us just 1 second to cross one. Finally we reached the version we were supposed to go. And when we entered it , we fell so hardly on the ground.

" Thank goodness , you both are free from danger. " Said Shane

" It's good we all are here "

" Noah , have you counted that so much than you forgot how to do it know ? "

" Please repeat that , Brad "

" Jennie and Paxton aren't here. We are 6. "

" Oh no ! Where are they ? "

" They went before you so they were supposed to reach here earlier than you. Also it was more than 140 seconds they were in. "

So Jennie and Paxton couldn't make it till here. It was not long ago we met but I really felt sorry for them and almost was on verge of crying. I wondered what would have happened to them , did they mixed up the count or forgot to do that thing with leg on step 28. We also didn't know whether they are in some other version on dead.

" I wish , wherever they are. They are at peace. " I said emotionally.

Due to this sad news , I didn't actually noticed what's in my surroundings and what's different about this world. But when I did notice , I could kept my eyes away from it like I literally forgotted to blink.

If one is taking about heaven , he must be talking about this . This place was not less than that.

" Now , take us back to our version fast " said Jaelyn.

" What ! Take a deep breath girl . We just came here. I needed to rest , meet my people and then will start working on the project. It's not as easy as boiling a glass of water. " Said Eric.

" How long this would take ? "

" Do you actually have forgotten , Jaelyn ? "

" What now ? "

" The door could only be opened every three years. So chill here for some time. "

" Three years is not some time , Eric. "

" See , we can't change the rule of nature. But I would try to find an alternative to help you go back fast. I got many scientists friends and new technologies. Maybe we could find a way "

" You freaking idiot , just let us out of here. What about our families , our career . You have spoiled it all. We lost 3 people and these could be us too." Said Brad.

" And all for what , so that a weird scientist guy who studies multiverse could go back to his own world. A guy who doesn't care about people , who uses them for their own purpose. One who have separated families. What we even have done to you ever that you make our life sucked " said Noah.

" You are a murderer , a kidnaper and god knows what else."

" I am not that insensitive as you portrayed me. Just imagine yourself in my shoes. Then you could understand my pain. "

" We even can't imagined to be that evil so that we can be in your shows " said Brad.

" Stop you all , now I will say and you all will listen . I should get a chance to tell my side of story too. "

CHAPTER X

Other Side Of Coin

" You are calling me murderer , kidnaper etc. but you don't even have an idea what I have went through. "

" I don't care what you have gone through , I only cared about how you tricked us to come here " said Brad.

Eric take us to a different place where he gave us some food and we all sat down. He really want to spoke his heart out that day.

" Tell , what you want to say now. " Said Noah.

" I was just five years old when my father died through brain cancer. Me , my elder brother named Nick and my mom were left all alone. My mom didn't have enough money to bear all are expenses. I don't even have the count of nights I have slept without eating anything.

So my mother married my step father. He used to paid our school fees and everything. He already had a son named Ryan. My step father and Ryan both used to tourture us everyday but we could do anything in response because we were buried under their favours. We just had to keep our heads down before them.

My family was physically tortured in front of my eyes but my hands were tied. We had to follow everything they say without saying a word.

They used to own a science firm of research and development. They forced me and Nick to study the same course so that we can work under them in firm. Years went by , I was living my terrible life.

Over a course of time , the behaviour of Ryan and my step father started changing in a good way. I was growing a sort of respect for them .

I was almost 22 when I started working in their firm. Ryan was already working there for not more than 3 years then. We both were now physically strong so maybe that's why they stopped beating us and started treated us in a good way but I was completely wrong.

They were using us for their game in which we were their puppet.

They tricked us into giving a big project . They told me that it is one of the greatest project that firm has worked on and they were giving us this opportunity to lead it.

They was no boundations of happiness we were feeling then. We were so thankful to Ryan and our step father that we can't see their runs under their tongues.

The project was related to parallel universe and all about it. For two years I completely got lost in the project. While eating , bathing and everytime I used to think about it. Our work was to find a possibility that a person could travel through this different worlds.

By working day and night , me and Nick were successful in doing so.

We told Ryan that the project is done. He congratulated us and also throwed a party. Meanwhile , this news was all over that our firm has achieved this but all the credit was given to Ryan. Our names weren't mentioned even once. He was getting awards for this.

Me and Nick confronted Ryan and our step father. But they completely denied to gave us anything and told us that we are born to work under their shoes with head down everytime.

We were almost on a verge to beat them so hardly that they can't even imagine but our mother don't let us do so. She blackmailed us that she would killed herself if we gave any harm to them.

They told us that our next task is to reach their. We weren't ready to do it and told them that we only know how to go there but not how to came back. Then they told us it we didn't know how to came back that stay there only.

That was the moment that they knew , we would do something . So they were already prepared for it. They had hid our mother somewhere and if didn't do as they say they would have killed her.

Somehow ,Nick managed to find a solution to came back but they was a little chance it would work as we had so much little time to think about it.

Overnight , Ryan stole the research documents in which the process of coming back was there one day before of our departure. But he didn't agreed that he did so. Nick didn't remember the process for it completely and we knew we were screwed.

If we didn't do it , we can't see our mom again. If we did it , there's a little probability of us coming back here in our world.

While we were entering the gate we formed to enter other universe, I heard a gun shot. Ryan killed Nick. His bodyguards hold me tightly that I wasn't able to moved.

He knew that only Nick knew the method as he didn't want us to came back. And why would he be , he has so much hatred for us since so long. His father replaced his mother , and marries ours. His friends used to bully him because of this . He wasn't allowed to meet his mom or his real sister who stayed with her mom only. He believed it's all because of us but we didn't have any role in it.

Maybe beating us everyday, stealing our archivements weren't enough for him that he killed my brother and then with the help of his bodyguards forced me to go into hole.

Remember I told you that my partner knew how to reach here, that partner was my brother , my life.

So entered your world alone , I had a translating device through which I studied your language. I worked so hard here , newspaper delivery in the morning , pizza delivery in daytime , and watchman shift in evening.

There wasn't a single night in almost 3 years that I hadn't worked on building this remote. But these weren't enough , the money I used to get was so less and technology applicines I required was so costly.

I started stealing , that's the only thing I could do. I even when to jail once but came out within a week because I gave some share of the money I stole to that police man who was handling my case. Greedy people , you know.

Soon I had a fair amount of money. I started making connections with scientists of your version . With the help of technology they provided, this remote was built.

I also researched about how I could travel back and did that too. I only used to sleep 2 hours a day and hardly used to had some food because I didn't want to waste any time. They was fire of revenge burning in my heart all this years.

If I didn't have find the solution, I would have to wait another three years for opening of that gate. Then you knew everything, how I used your place and all. I am sorry I did that but I was not like this before. My circumstances forced me to be the person I am now.

People have only used my kindness for their own purposes. Seeing my brother and father death in front of me , Seeing my mother got tortured by her new husband, Seeing myself get hurt everyday , bullied everyday , made me so stone hearted that I no longer had feelings. I had become a walking dead .

Only purpose that I am still alive is to save my mother and makes sure my step father and Ryan feel same what I have felt all these years.

Again I apologise for whatever I did to you guys , I promise I will amend my mistake and you will be home soon "

After hearing Eric's story , we weren't able to move or say anything. My thinking of him completely changed . The struggle of him was so intense. We felt sorry for whatever happened to him and told him that we would try to coperate with him.

We went to a old house where he used to live earlier before her mother marries his step father. The place was stinking and dirty. We cleaned it completely and rest their for a while.

CHAPTER XI

Mission Revenge

" Where you are going ? " Asked Shane

" I need to know where my mom is , I am going to theirs house. "

" Are you sure , they still be leaving there after 3 years ? "

" 3 years went in your version , but it's only been 3 months in ours."

Sometimes , it was hard to understand what Eric said. After discussing it over for 15 minutes, we finally understood. These different versions have different time theory too. 1 year in our version is 1 month here.

In every version it's different. It's called time lapse theory or something.

" I'll come with you too " said Brad.

" No , I don't want to trouble you more. It's because of you guys only I am back home. You just rest , I'll handle everything. Don't go out from here , It could be risky "

" Comeon , you can't do it all alone. You could also get caught if Ryan sees you "

Eric agreed to let us helped him . He gave the translation band which we put on so we could understand what people here are saying.

We made a plan so that we could get a idea of where Eric's mom is kept by his family.

Jaelyn stayed at Eric's old house only as she usually panics in these situations. Brad and Eric went to Ryan his father's house. Me , Noah and Shane went to the science firm they own to keep an eye on Ryan.

" Did you and Jaelyn talked ? " Asked Shane

" Yeah , we talked. "

" So you sort everything? "

" I tried but she said we'll be back to normal if I stopped talking to Tracy from now on. "

" What ? " Both me and Shane said it at the same time.

" I also had the same reaction. Now close the big mouth you opened , it's weird "

" So you agreed to it ? " Said Shane

" I could never agreed to it in any universe. "

" Idiot , do as she say . Save your relationship, it's best for you both. Don't worry about me , I will not die if I didn't talk to you . Also who want to talk to you anyway. " I said

" No , I won't . She didn't even believe my loyalty towards her. So now I'll be loyal to my friends. And please let's focus on our revenge mission , no more discussion on this topic "

I was stunned after Noah told me that. All I was thinking was what things I have done in past that made Jaelyn insecure. My mind said that , I should try to mediate between both of them but heart always wants different things. I knew that , this feeling was one sided.

As we were wandering through the city , I noticed that it's almost same as ours. Greenery on the sidewalks, automatic cars and shops , cleanliness at its peak and many other things which we saw first time.

Following the city's map , we reached the science firm where Ryan was supposed to work at that time.

Eric had already told us everything about it. The place had 3 gates - 1 in back and 1 in front covered with security guards and 1 secret gate which only few knew about.

Our work was to enter the firm through secret gate which would take us to a duct, there we had to bring a green colour file from the office room. Eric told us it's the file his brother and he make during their research.. But there was again a problem, the file was protected and could only be taken out if you solved a puzzle and enter the correct answer on it . Out of sympathy for Eric , we agreed to helped him but the work is not as simple and fun as I thought it would.

" Why have we agree to help him ? " Said Shane.

" We have to gain his trust. Otherwise I don't think he will work hardly to take us back home. If we will help him , in return he has to definitely do the same. " Said Noah

" What if he don't do the same ? "

" Well , I have thought about that too. We will help him but side by side will collect proofs against him , like now he made do this stealing and etc. Then , if he flipped at the last moment, we could blackmailed him."

" Isn't it wrong ? He trusted us "

" We should always have our one step ahead. We will not broke his trust , if he don't broke ours. If he started working on our project and be successful, I will bury these proofs that I would be collecting on my way"

I didn't feel Noah was doing right at that time. I felt like we shouldn't question Eric's loyalty.

" He promised us that we will get home, so he would do the same ." I said

" I know but what's even wrong about me doing this. It will be positive for us rather than negative "

" Noah , what if he get to know about it ? "

" I will hide it , nobody's going to know . It's between three of us and better be. "

" Yes , Tracy . Take a chill pill. Noah's plan could help us in long term. So just go along with it " said Shane.

We found the gate , and were travelling through the duct to find the office room. As we were moving across it , we saw different persons and rooms in between. In one room , a old man and 28 year something person was sitting across the table having a deep discussion.

" It could be Ryan and his father " I whispered.

Ryan was a handsome and muscular man. His father look very pale due to old age.

I tried to heard what they were saying but these ducts were build at a great height from the room. Due to which I was unable to do so.

I wondered if they had any idea that Eric was back.

" We have to find out the office room fast. We are taking so much time " said Shane

The Duct was not strong enough to carry all our weight and it got broke. We fell down but fortunately in the office room where the file was kept. We made a loud noise when we fell down .

" Hide away ! Someone could come here after hearing our scream. "

5 minutes went by and we were hiding but no one came. We thought nobody had heard it . So we continued our work.

We tap the button on the box where file was kept. A map and a pen came out of it. In map rooms and even tables were given a number to represent it. On pen a maths statement was written. It was understandable that we had to first solved the equation then go to place corresponding to that number.

" Wish I didn't have bunked my Maths classes. " Said Shane

" Well , finally I know where trigonometry is used in real life " Said Noah

" Why aren't you solving it ? " I said

" Nice joke , Tracy. Did you forget me and Shane always came first in maths class but from last ? "

All the pressure then fall onto me. I was average in maths. Eventually not only in Maths but I was average in every field of work. Usually I reliased this in night when I tried to sleep. Everyone was best in artistic things have different hobbies except me.

" Don't think, just solve "

" Then do it yourself, Shane "

" Okay , try number 75 "

It was wrong. We entered 5 more numbers but all were wrong.

" I shouldn't have high expectations from you " said Shane

" I don't even remember last time I studied this topic , still I am trying unlike you just Standing there and staring my face "

I didn't want to failed . So i tried one more time .

" Try 89 now "

It worked , we hugged each other out of happiness.

Suddenly alarm started buzzing.

Chuck - Chuck

We heard a sound like someone was opening the door knob. It happened so fast that we couldn't hide and get caught.

" Who are you ? What are you doing here ? " Said a man who look like a scientist only.

CHAPTER XII

Who To Trust ?

" Hello ! Actually we came here to meet someone but got lost. " Said Noah

" If is that so , then why this duct is broken, and why there's this green file in your hand " said that Man.

We didn't have any other excuse to make . We were caught and messed up everything.

Noah punched that man , grab the file and shouted run. We ran through the firm to reach the secret gate from where we entered but failed and security guards caught us.

They took us to the office where Ryan and his father were present. Our game was almost over.

" Gave us your introduction " said Ryan.

" I am Noah , he is Shane and this is Tracy. "

" Why are you here ? "

" Actually we are homeless and were in urgent need of money. A man told us that if brought this file to him , he will gave us some money." Said Noah.

God ! He was so good at lying.

" Who was that man ? "

" We met him first time only "

We kept on answering Ryan's question about how we enter , and how we solved the maths equation to open the lock.

" Where you came from ? " Asked Ryan

" We lived here only on different foothpath " said Shane

" What's this city name ? "

We got frozen. We didn't know the name and if we say so he won't believe.

" How would you know even , you don't belong from here . "

" Looking at the clothes you are wearing ,the way you speak ,and your physique anybody here could guessed." Said Ryan's father.

" So where's Eric ? " Asked Ryan

" Who's Eric ? " Said Shane.

" No more lies please otherwise you won't be in a condition to speak "

We couldn't figured out what to do next. There's no other option than to speak the truth. There was a gun on our head.

" Bring the electric chair " Ryan ordered his one guard.

" We will tell you everything. Please don't do it " I said .

" Yeah , you will have to. If you say a single lie you will get shock so be careful "

The guard brought 3 chairs and made us sit on it. Ryan started asking us different questions and we answered it all. Noah get a shock when he tried to lie about Eric.

We were scared about our future. Eric could now easily be caughted because of information we provided. And we will stuck in this version without Eric

A man came from behind and whispered something in Ryan's ear which made him so nervous.

" What happen son ? "

" Papa , Eric stoled the original file "

" Wasn't security there , Ryan ? "

" Everyone was here only with these guys "

Eric asked everybody to seal the building, call police and spread around to find Eric.

" Can you please tell us what's happening ?"

" It was all Eric's gameplan. He send you to take the fake file so that you got caught and all attention goes to you. Meanwhile he came and stole the original one without even anyone noticing ".

" He is doing all this for us so that we could go back to our universe. "

" The file states the making of one of the biggest and most dangerous atomic bomb. Thats why we kept it hidden. "

" Why would Eric do that ? "

" You are literally emotional fools. Can't you see , he used you. All the stories he told you was completely fake. "

We were so shocked that we made a fool of ourselves. Ryan told us that Eric was a pyscho murderer. He had murdered his real brother because he was just jealous of us.

He soon became a most wanted criminal after killing his brother. So he escaped and travelled through to the other version so that no one could found him.

They don't know the reason he came back. They also mentioned that they hide his mother because he could killed anyone.

According to them , they were completely opposite of what Eric told us. He show us a video where Eric tried to killed them also and he experimenting dangerous chemicals.

He was a egoistic person who wanted control over the world. Whoever tried to stopped him in doing so , he would just killed him. He built some kinds of arms because of we he usually escaped from the hands of police.

" At this moment , I doubt we could trust you or not " I said.

" Think practically, If he wanted to help you , why would he send you here to take the fake file . He knew you will get caught and we will not leave you then."

" We don't care about what is right or what is wrong. My head is spinning " said Shane.

" We have to catch Eric and only you could help us . He got that file and could blow up everything "

" Ryan , First we have to save our friends - Brad and Jaelyn. They must be with Eric only. He could mistreat them . Let's check his old house where Jaelyn was." said Noah.

" He is not that stupid that he will kept your friend there only. That's the most obvious place he could be. And he doesn't do obvious things. "

Other guard came and told us that Eric is nowhere to be seen. They have checked his old palce and no one was there not even Jaelyn. Our blood pressure literally started rising and we we couldn't think of anything.

" I am releasing you three. I remember a place where he could be"

" So send your guards there "

" He is looking over everything through CCTV cameras. Till now he must have hacked them all. There's no camera in here , that's why we are able to talk freely. He would see guards coming over there and he would eventually run away. "

We decided that we three would act like we break free from the firm and are free. We would wander through the city to found help and Eric would noticed us through different cameras.

When we would arrived at his old house , we would say few things on the camera. After hearing those , Eric would came to us directly.

While we kept Eric busy with us , few guards would enter the woods in a different appearance. As according to Ryan , there's this old tree house where they used to play as kids. It's in between the woods. That's the only place where there is no CCTV camera and Eric could be there.

Doing the same , we arrived the old house and started saying few things over the camera of main entrance. In this version, there is cameras almost everywhere.

" Hey Eric , are you hearing us ? We managed to escaped from the firm. They were busy looking for you and we took the advantage of the situation. " Said Noah looking at the camera.

" We have also brought the file with us. We can't find you . Please help us , where are you. We are waiting for you here . One important thing , we have found something else there which could help you to take your revenge from them. There this bag we found. It have many explosives and chemical solutions . It was kept protected so we thought it must be something important " I said.

We thought that this plan won't worked . Eric was a smart person , he won't get caught in our plan. But I was wrong. Greed could made someone do anything.

Eric got greedy after seeing that bag which had fake explosives and solutions. Ryan had given us that beforehand.

CHAPTER XIII

Hey Eric

While we were waiting there in Eric's old house , guard went to the woods to find the treehouse.

We heard a knock on the door and was convinced that it maybe someone else but not Eric. I opened the door and Eric was standing there staring at my eyes.

" It's good you guys are fine " said Eric.

" Yeah , you came and distract them . Due to which we did this. Thank you Eric. "

" I couldn't leave you there alone right , Tracy . "

" What about Jaelyn and Brad ? ".

" They are absolutely fine , Noah "

Eric took the bag away from us and gave us some big jackets and cap to wear. We followed him to a car which took us to middle of the woods. That was the same tree house which Ryan told us about. We climb the stairs to reach the house. It was very dark and I felt like someone twisted my hand.

Eric handcuffed us. He on the lights and I saw Brad and Jaelyn across the house in same situation as us.

" What you are doing ? " Asked Shane.

" Thank you for everything you guys. Because of you I could came back here. Because of you I could get that file. Because of you I get another bag of explosives "

" We thought you were nice person "

" Ohh Brad , there's no term like nice person which exists in the world. This universe is full of devils and you just meet one. "

" You broke our trust , Eric . "

" Yeah , I did. It was your mistake to trust me. I am most wanted criminal in here , I came to your version to save myself because I was almost weak. I enjoyed there and came back to show everyone who I am. I never run , I am always behind looking a moment for stab. Like how I killed my brother. And that story in tell you was false. I was not being bullied , I was the bully. "

" Please save us , take us back to our version . We will be forever greatful to you " requested Jaelyn.

" I never wanted people to be grateful to me. I want their soul burning whenever they heard my name "

" We helped you with so many things . Can't you just returned the favour. "

" No , my dear Brad. But I could gave a favour to specially you. You will be the last one to get killed among your friends. "

My bones shivered after this. I didn't expected my life to turn this way.

" First care about your life , brother" said Ryan with a while army behind him downstairs.

" I got my first prey"

Eric shot his gun but there was no bullet inside it .

" My man have already taken it out. You should be more attentive. Thanks Brad for doing it . Now it's my turn " said Ryan.

Ryan shot the gun right in Eric's leg. He started to bleed. Ryan called the guards and they take him to the hospital. He opened our handcuffs we were free.

" I thought you won't be coming "

" How come I won't . You get a chance like this only once. "

Ryan booked us a hotel room for few days while Eric got arrested. We weren't still sure if we could go back.

A week went by , we haven't heard anything from Ryan. We tried to contact him with the help of hotel staff there.

Finally we found his number and asked him to meet us as he was our last hope . We just prayed he didn't ditched us after his work is done.

" Hey , how you doing ? "

" No that great "

" Why ? This place isn't comfortable "

" But this place is nowhere close to home. We are missing our family. "

" For that , I have a bad news and a good news too . I'll will tell you later until it's confirmed. "

" What about Eric ? "

" He had a remote like device with him . With the help of it he vanished. "

" Where ? How could you let him vanish ? "

" We didn't knew about the remote . He could be anywhere now , maybe again in some other version. I had to tell you this. Wherever you are, try to be safe. You never knew when he came back. "

After this, even if we go back , we can't leave peacefully because of this stupid Eric.

Ryan went back and told us he will come back tomorrow with a solution for us. He had also gave 2 guards duty to protect us if Eric came to us.

" Jaelyn , I get to know what you said to Noah regarding our friendship. I am completely fine with it . You guys should be together and I will not come in between, neither I have ever came. "

" I would like to hear those words from Noah not you. It doesn't matter if you are fine with it or not "

Noah jumped into the conversation from nowhere.

" You will never heard those words then. Tracy is one of my closest friend and I won't leave her alone. And why would I be back with you , you don't have faith in me . What if you started doing the same with my other friends too. I will not let you control my life in any way ".

" It's the end of our stupid relationship " said Jaelyn

" I am glad. " Noah smashed the room door and went outside.

Shane signed me to go behind Noah while he and Brad sat with Jaelyn. I started seeing our group spilliting away.

At this moment, where we should be with each other and support each other , we were fighting.

Jaelyn and I were only girls in the group. We used to share a strong bond which is fading away slowly and slowly.

My heart was aching. My life would never be the same as it was.

I saw Noah near the water fountain of the hotel. As I went near him , I noticed he was crying. I put my hand over his shoulder. He turn around and started crying even more.

I hugged him by the water fountain. We both were shedding tears. Then had a deep conversation for over 3 hours. We didn't even noticed we kept talking this long.

Then a hotel staff member came and told us someone had come to meet us.

CHAPTER XIV

Lose Or Lose

We followed the staff member to our room. It was Ryan who was waiting for us. He told us he will come tomorrow but he was there before time. We thought maybe he got a good news which he came to tell us .

" You were supposed to come tomorrow. Is everything alright ? "

" Eric is around only. He will come to kill one of you. He left this letter where he said this. He also mentioned he will leave a choice upto you so that one of you could surender. Other could go back to their version as he only had the knowledge to do it. "

" Tight the security. How come he reached here ? "

" We had a deal with him, that if he take you back , his punishment would be less . He also knows that it's a waste to run now. We have found his other base and destroyed everything. He can't run to any version now. He is all over TV. Thousands of police is looking for him. Every citizen of the country is looking for him. "

" So just found him , and asked us to send us all . Why he want to kill one of us ? "

" I told you , he is a pyscho murderer. He is so persistent , he will take as much as pain we gave him but will not let you go back until we fulfilled what he want. He wants one of you and it you want to go home then choose one between you otherwise you all stay here only for forever. "

" No one would die within us " said Noah.

" One more thing , if you are going to stayed here , you have stayed in jail for the rest of your life. According to the rules , you are regarded as aliens here and you can't be let free. I have talked with government but they didn't agreed. I have 4 hours from them. Within this you have to decide whether to stayed in jail for lifetime here or go back but without one of your friends. "

We were stuck between the devil and the deep blue sea. Either way , we were losing only.

" Litsen , let me surrender myself. Earlier also you didn't let me do. " Said Noah

" We're going to jail. " Said Shane.

" No , it's easy to say. But it would be so difficult. And by giving my life , you guys could lived happily "

" Noah , without you there will be no happiness in my life. "

" We can't do it this way. After you , Brad would say he will go , then I will come forward. We all are ready to gave our lives for each other. That's why it's difficult to choose. "

" You are correct, Jaelyn. "

" It's the same situation we were in before when pilot got inside the hole. " Said Brad

" It's better to go to jail. I can't lose anybody".

" Shane , one day everyone had to die . Some die earlier, some late. It doesn't matter"

" If it doesn't matter , then let me go , Noah"

" Let's vote. If majority say we should be in jail , we would be there only for forever but together " said Shane.

We did voting , everyone voted for going to jail. We could see our future in front of us.

Ryan told us he will come within an hour to litsen to our decision .

We all were tensed. Nobody said a word.

Ryan came in after an hour .

" It was a good decision to safe 4 of you " said Ryan.

" We haven't told you about our decision yet. Why you are assuming we are letting one of us die ? "

" You don't know about that ? Haven't you noticed Brad's not there in the room since an hour. "

My jaw dropped. None of us noticed when Brad left the room. We all were so quiet all this time and doesn't even saw what was happening around us.

" Where is he ? Bring him back please" Said Noah.

" He can't came back now. Government officials would have taken him by now to Eric."

" How could he decide that himself ? " I said

" He told me it's a mutual decision. That's why I let him do it. Now get ready to go home. "

" I won't leave without him . We decided that we would be at jail. He can't do this to us. Stop it. Call the officials, I want to talk to him "

Ryan told us that he would take us to the place where Brad was being taken. While we reached there , damage had already been done. We saw officials taking Brad's dead body. One of that person came to us and gave us a letter from Brad.

We weren't even in state of mind to read that. We run and clinged to his body. We all were crying. It felt time stopped around us. Everything seems frozen. We lost our Brad.

" Braddddd , My friend. Please come back. He is alive . Call the doctor. " Screamed Shane.

" No he isn't " said Ryan.

" Why you did this Brad ? Please don't go. Please don't go. Nothing happened to you , you are fine. Open your eyes. " Said Noah

Officials kicked us away from his body. We saw Eric in front of us. He was handcuffed and was smiling. We all just attacked him, he was completely in blood , but police tied us .

" Brad have gave his life so that you could go back and you are beating Eric. You know he is the only person who could do it. "

Brad body was taken by police for funeral. We weren't allowed to be in the process.

" He told me before dying , he really want you to read his letter. Don't forget about it . It's his last wish " said one of the police officer.

My tears weren't stopping.

" It's all because of me. We lost our brother, our friend , our everything " said Noah.

CHAPTER XV

The Letter

Hello my sweethearts

You must be reading this while I'll be gone. I am really sorry I didn't respected our decision to go to jail. I am writing this while i am in a police car travelling to my death.

I am starting having flashbacks of my life and you guys are the best memory of it.

I was a orphan who you guys kind of adopted. Where ever I would fight with my Brother, I used to left his home and came to you.

Whenever I needed you guys were there. Noah helped me pay my college fees . Jaelyn would always helped me with my homework. Sometimes she used to did mine also. Tracy always used to motivate me wherever I was feeling low because of my family problems. And Shane you were my bestfriend , I always crashed to your house. I used to make fun of you but you never take my silly things on heart.

I could never do anything for you guys. Always was a burden on this world. First to my brother who kicked me out of the house , then to you.

Now it's my turn to something for you.

My life isn't as important as yours . I didn't have any other family other than you. You guys have parents who are waiting for you to come home .

You guys told me what it feels like to be in family . I am so thankful for that

I had few last wishes that you had to fulfilled.

No-1) I know it's hard to forget me because I am so special. But promise me you guys would move on without me . Don't think of staying in jail here.

No-2) Don't have any regrets. It's not because of any of you. It's just what god wants or maybe karma which I deserved .

No-3) When you go back , you have to live your life to the fullest. Enjoy every moment because you never know when you met another Eric who will make your life hell.

No-4) Don't let anyone take my place. I wanted to be alive in your hearts. So make some room in your heart where I can live peacefully.

No-5) No matter whatever happens between you , you would meet once in a while. Don't loose connection with each other . Always meet at the booth we all used sit together.

No-6) Even if Jaelyn and Noah is having a breakup , you guys have to stay best friends. You would also be better of as friends like me and Jaelyn.

No-7) Nobody would cry. I hate tears you know.

I know its too many last wishes but you guys had to do this favour for me.

Now just get ready, this trip is over. Our version is waiting.

One more thing , I love you guys so much like from the moon to the sun covering all versions.

You are the only best I have ever done in my life. Go ahead with you career and be successful.

One last thing , always be happy. I know I won't be there to make you laugh with my silly jokes but now you have to live without it only.

Be yourself and love yourself

I love you all

Goodbye ,

Your Brad.

There was nothing left to say now.

"Why life is like this?" Asked Noah.

" Its like a heartbeat. We all have our ups and downs. When the life become straight like when everything happens the way we wanted , our heartbeat also becomes straight which symbolises our death. So while we are leaving , we have to live with ups and downs.

Because we know what happens when it all got straight "

About the book :-

We all sometimes In our life must heard about parallel universe which literal meaning is A reality or world that exists simultaneously with ours, but independent of it.

But we never believed something like this to actually exist same like our 5 friends - Noah , Tracy , Jaelyn , Shane and Brad .

But a plane flight clear their doubts when they meet a mysterious person on their way to Europe.

This book deceipts about their horrible trip which they would never forget and their struggles in finding their own self.

About the author:-

Heyy !

Myself Medha Suneja and I am a teenager. This is the first book I ever written , I had this story in my mind for so long but never had the audacity to write about it. But now I want you to enter in a whole different world through my book which I hope you liked .

Printed by Libri Plureos GmbH in Hamburg,
Germany

9 798887 045344